KU-016-013

Footprints in the Snow

Contents

The Crash

It happened last December,
one bitterly cold night.
We were driving back from a party –
Floyd, Karen and me –
when it started to snow.

We didn't care about the weather.
The car heater kept us warm.
We'd be home in an hour or so.

But the snow grew thicker.
Soon it was bouncing off the windscreen
and I could hardly see where we were going.
I leaned forward, gripping the steering wheel.
I stared ahead as the road twisted
through the mountains.

'Have a break, Mike,' said Karen.
'Let me drive for a bit.'

I should have stopped.
I was exhausted and my eyes were blinded
by the dazzle from the snow.
But I didn't stop. I went on.
That was my big mistake.
We were miles from anywhere.
Then it happened.
That terrible accident. I shall never forget.
Of course I should have been more careful.
The road was narrow – it was so easy to skid.

But I didn't think.
I was dog-tired and still driving. Stupid!
Suddenly headlights leapt out of the dark.

'Look out!' Floyd yelled.

I swung away from the oncoming car.
We swerved off the tarmac …
Lights flashed … Glass shattered … CRASH!
I heard the deafening noise of metal buckling.
Then silence.

Slowly, I raised my head.

I could see that we'd smashed into a tree.

I had a sore neck – nothing more.

But what about the others?

As I turned, an icy blast tore through

the broken windscreen.

It took my breath away.

'Are you two OK?' I gasped.

Floyd grunted from the back seat.

'My leg hurts like mad!' he said.

Karen hadn't said anything.

I turned to look at her, sitting next to me.

Her chin was flopped against her chest.

Was she still alive?

I leaned over to get a closer look.

'She's breathing,' I said,

as I saw her lips move.

'Pass my anorak from the back seat, Floyd.

We've got to keep her warm.'

I laid the padded jacket over her thin dress.

Snowflakes had begun to settle on her face

and hair.

'It'll soon be like a fridge in here,' I said.
'We've got to get help.'

'Right,' said Floyd. 'I've got my mobile.
I'll dial 999.'
He reached into his jacket pocket,
switched it on and waited.
'I can't get a signal,' he said.
I groaned. 'Are the mountains blocking it?'
He stared at the display panel.
'No,' he said sheepishly. 'The battery's flat.'

Angrily, I climbed out of the car.
I had to do something.
As I stood peering through the snow,
the freezing wind ripped at my sweater.
I looked, hoping to see the other car.
Maybe it had stopped further down the road.
No such luck.
Even its tyre marks had disappeared.

The night was silent, except for the wind
in the trees. No sound of distant traffic.
Nothing. We could all freeze to death
before anyone came to help.

House on the Hill

As I stood there, I saw something
that made my pulse race.
There were footprints in the snow!
Three sets crossing the road. Fantastic!
Someone must have gone that way
in the last few minutes.

I traced the footprints up the bank opposite.
Then, through the trees
I saw something at the top of the hill.
It was a house – and its lights were blazing.
Someone was home!

I hurried back to the others.
'I'm going for help,' I said,
leaning into the car.
As I did so, I noticed Karen's eyes were open.
'Karen!' I said. 'You all right?'
She looked up at me and I saw that her lips
were blue with cold.
She smiled weakly.
'I don't think I can walk, Mike,' she said.
'And I can't stop shaking.
I need to get warm.'

She was right. She couldn't stay in the car.
She wouldn't last long in these temperatures.

I had to get her up to that house somehow.
'How bad's your leg, Floyd?' I asked.
'Can you manage to walk if I carry Karen?'
He nodded. 'I'll manage,' he said.
'Just find me a stick or something to lean on.'
I looked around the trunk of the tree.
There were broken branches everywhere
and I soon found one for him.
'I'll wrap my scarf around the top,' I said.
'You can tuck it under your arm.'

I turned and reached for Karen.
I knew I shouldn't move her.
But I had no choice. She'd die of cold
if I didn't get her inside soon.
Would I be able to carry her
all the way up the hill?
Already, my hands were blocks of ice.
'Don't worry, Mike!' she whispered
as I wrapped my arms around her.
'We'll make it.'
But as I lifted her out of the car,
I heard her gasp in pain.

'Hold on, Karen,' I said. 'I'll get you up
to that nice warm house. No problem.'

The snow was now falling thicker than ever.
It clung to my cheeks and my eyelashes.
I struggled on.
Karen was a dead weight in my arms.
'Keep going!' I said to myself over and over.
'Keep going!'

I fixed my eyes on the house.
'Nearly … there,' I panted.
'Come … on … Floyd!'
There was no reply.
He must have fallen behind –
but I daren't look back.

Finally we reached the house,
and I sat Karen carefully on the step –
grateful to be free of the weight.
Then I grasped the knocker and rapped loudly.
No one came. I tried again. Nothing.
In desperation, I turned the handle.
'Anybody home?' I shouted as the door opened.

I stepped into the hall.
'Hello!' I called. No reply.

I looked downstairs.
I shouted up the stairs. But no one was there.
I hurried back to the front door.
'The place is empty!' I said.
'But I've got to get you inside.
I'm sure the owners won't mind.
It's an emergency, isn't it?'

Karen nodded. 'I expect they'll be back soon,'
she said. 'We'll explain.'

Gently, I picked her up
and laid her on the settee.
'Thanks, Mike,' she whispered.
'You were brilliant.'
She closed her eyes, groaning softly.

As I bent down to switch on the electric fire,
I saw a photo on the mantelpiece.
It was of a man and woman with a little girl.
'They must be the owners,' I said.

Drowsily, Karen grunted in agreement.
I wanted to stay with her
but I was worried about Floyd.

I wrote a note to the owners in case Karen
was asleep when they got back.
Then I walked out of the front door
and into the blizzard.
I peered down the slope.
But I could see nothing through the snow.
'Floyd,' I shouted against the wind.
'Floyd, where are you?'
There was no reply.
I set off into the cold night once more.

Where's Floyd?

I stumbled through the snow,
slipping and falling as I went.
My clothes were wet and caked in snow.
There was still no sign of Floyd.

'Floyd,' I yelled, beginning to panic.
I stood still and listened for a reply.
Was that a groan?
I waited and heard the sound again.
It had to be him. He must have fallen.

'Floyd!' I shouted. 'Keep making a noise
so I can find you! Don't give up!'

I heard just one small moan
and then silence.

No matter how I called after that,
there was never a reply.
Slowly I moved forward towards the road.
My body was shaking with cold and fear.
All this was my fault.
My two best friends were injured –
all because I'd been too tired to drive.
Too proud to let Karen take the wheel.
'Please let me find Floyd,' I prayed.
'Don't let him die out here.'

I staggered on.
It was only by luck that I tripped
on something across my path.
It was a branch with my scarf around it!
It was Floyd's stick! He couldn't be far away.
I began to crawl around
on my hands and knees.
I patted the snow. I shouted. I yelled.
And then my hand struck
a soft lump of clothes.
A heap lying on the ground.
I had found him. It was Floyd.

The Mystery Car

I pulled Floyd up to a sitting position.
His eyes were closed.
His head lolled to one side like a rag doll.

'Wake up, Floyd!' I shouted, shaking him.
You can't give in. I've found you now!'

Slowly, his eyes opened and he looked at me.
'Mike!' he said softly as if in a dream.

I managed to get him to stand.
Then I tucked the stick under his right arm
and put his left arm around my shoulder.
Neither of us had much strength left.

The way up to the house seemed impossible.
But somehow we managed to get there.
As we closed the door behind us,
Floyd moaned with pain and relief.
So now we were all safe inside the house.
But the owners still had not returned.

'We need to dry off,' I said.
'Do you think they'd mind if we borrowed
some towels?'

I went upstairs to find some.
At the top was a door with the word KAY
in wooden letters.
Next to it was a tall cupboard
full of sheets and towels.
Floyd and I stripped in front of the fire
and rubbed ourselves dry.

'We'll put our clothes on the hearth,' I said.
They'll be dry in no time.'

Floyd sat in the armchair,
wrapped in a large white towel.

'You know, Mike,' he said
staring at the glowing bars.
'I think I was going mad out there.'
'You just fell down the hill,' I said.
'No. I didn't fall,' he said.
'I turned back to the road.'
'Why?'
'Because I heard a car coming,' he said.
'I was going to flag it down. Get help.'
I sat on the corner of the hearth
and looked up at him.
'I saw a pair of headlights,' he said.
'So there was a car!'
'Not exactly.'

It didn't make sense.
What was he talking about?

'I could hear the noise of an engine,'
he explained.
'But there was no car behind the headlights.
You see what I mean …
Either this was some phantom car
or I'm going mad.'

The Webbs

We sat and waited for the owners to return.
Karen slept.
The house was strangely silent. Empty.
'I don't understand,' I said. 'Why walk out of
the house at this time of night?'
'Some emergency, maybe,' said Floyd
resting his leg on a chair.

'I wish they'd come back. My leg's killing me.'

'You both need a doctor,' I said.
'We can't wait any longer.
I'm going to ring for the ambulance.'

I went into the hall and found the phone
on a small table.

Next to it was a pile of letters
addressed to Mr and Mrs P Webb.

I lifted the handset to dial 999.
As I put it to my ear, I knew it was useless.
A silence told me the line was dead.

'The snow must have brought down the lines,'
said Floyd as I walked into the living room.

I shook my head. 'No. This place is weird.
I've got a bad feeling about it.
There's something not right.'

Floyd shrugged his shoulders.

'You're just feeling spooky tonight.

The cold must have got to your brain.'

Then he sank his head against the chair.

'I could really do with a cup of coffee, Mike.

Do you think you could make me one?'

I went into the kitchen and filled the kettle.

While I was waiting for it to boil,

I picked up a newspaper from the table

and turned to the front page.

I couldn't believe what I saw.

My blood ran cold

as I began to read the article.

ANOTHER DEATH AT DEVIL'S BEND

Locals say the phantom car is to blame.

A family of three was killed yesterday on the Brentmar Road. Peter and Jane Webb and their daughter, Kay, had been for a walk. They were crossing the road at the spot known as Devil's Bend. Hospital reports tell us they were knocked down by a car which did not stop. Their bodies were found by a patrol car. The police found no tyre marks or any evidence of the mystery car.

The name *Webb* –
it was on the letters on the hall table.
And the girl's name – *Kay* –
that was the name on the bedroom door.
My mind was racing. I read the article again
and then I looked at the picture underneath.
There was Mr and Mrs Webb
and their little girl.
A photo just like the one on the mantelpiece.

'Floyd!' I yelled, dashing across the hall.
'Read this!' And I handed him the paper.
'It's seriously weird.
The people who live here – they're dead!'

He struggled to sit up and read the article.
'I bet there's a simple explanation,' he said.
'Maybe a relative moved in here
after the accident. To tidy up.
Sell the house. You know.'
'I don't think so, Floyd,' I said,
pointing to the top of the front page.
'Haven't you noticed?
This paper is twenty years old.'

Karen Gets Worse

We were scared. But what could we do
except wait until daylight?

Floyd settled in the armchair.
I lay down on the floor.
Karen was sound asleep on the settee.

'Sleep's a great healer,' said Floyd.
'Karen will wake up in the morning
and she'll be fine.'

But Floyd was wrong. During the night,
the sound of Karen's breathing changed.
I got up and went to have a look at her.

'Karen,' I whispered. 'Are you all right?'
She didn't answer. Her breath was coming
in short gasps. Sometimes it grated.
Sometimes it rattled in her throat.
Floyd struggled to get up. 'She's choking,'
he said. 'Get her some water, Mike. Quick!'

I fetched a glass from the kitchen
and shook Karen gently by the shoulder.
'Karen, wake up,' I said. But she didn't.
'She's unconscious,' Floyd said. 'We shouldn't
move her. She's hurt worse than we thought.'
We wet her lips with the water and
made her as comfortable as we could.

'As soon as it's light,' I said,
'I'll go down to the road and start walking.'
'There isn't a town for miles,' said Floyd.
'There might be a house along the road,'
I said. 'I can ask to use their phone.'
I looked out of the window.
The snow was still falling.
I lay down on the floor and
soon sank into a deep exhausted sleep.

Footprints

I woke at first light.
I turned my head to look across at Karen –
dreading what I would see.
To my surprise, her eyes were open.
I sat bolt upright.
'Karen! How are you feeling?' I said.

She smiled at me. A strange distant smile.
'Fine,' she said. 'How are you two?'

'Floyd's leg's bad,' I said.
'But it's you we were worried about.
You were really ill last night.'

Slowly, she stood up.
'Thanks for looking after me, Mike,' she said.
'Thank you.'

I don't know what it was –
but there was something different about her.
Maybe it was the accident, I thought.

Floyd was in a deep sleep.
Karen and I went into the kitchen to talk.
I told her what we had found out.
The newspaper. The photo. Everything.
I remember how she just sat there.
As if she hadn't heard.
She just looked out of the window.

'At least it's stopped snowing,' she said.
'We can go home.'
'No,' I said. 'I'm going to walk
to the nearest town. I'll fetch help.'

But Karen had other ideas.
'I know a place near here,' she said.
'There's a village just over the hill.
We'll be there in ten minutes.'
'Ten minutes? Are you sure?'
'I'm sure.'

I was puzzled.
How come she knew this place so well?
We were miles from home.
Miles from anywhere.

It was at this point that
Floyd hobbled into the kitchen.
'Karen! You look brilliant!' he said.
'We thought you were a gonner last night.'
'Charming!' she said and laughed
that amazing laugh of hers.

We were so happy.
So relieved that we'd survived.
The snow had stopped
but the morning was bitterly cold.
Before we set off, we borrowed some coats
from the coatstand in the hall.
I remember how stupid Floyd and I looked.
The coats were too small, so we wrapped
them round our shoulders.
It was better than nothing.

Karen was a different matter.
She slipped a coat on and it fitted perfectly.
Then some gloves … and some boots.
It was as if they belonged to her.

'Right!' she said. 'All set. Let's go!'
She marched ahead, leading us
through the wood behind the house.
Floyd was hanging on to me.
His arm was around my shoulder as he
hobbled painfully through the snow.
It was hard going.

'Not so fast!' I yelled. 'We can't keep up.'
Suddenly, Karen raised her arm
and pointed to the right.
'Down that path,' she said.
'Through those trees.'

She knew exactly which way to go.
'The next bit's hard,' she called
as she waited for us to catch up.
'There's a steep slope here.
Do you think you can manage?'

'How much further?' I panted.
'Floyd's finding it tough going.
He's in a lot of pain.'
'Nearly there,' she said.
'The village is in the valley.'
She was right. We saw the houses
as soon as we reached the brow of the hill.

'We made it!' I shouted.
'You were brilliant, Karen!'
She smiled a pale distant smile.
'You'll be OK now,' she said softly.
With that she turned
and walked towards the trees.
I stared open mouthed. 'Karen!' I yelled.
'Where are you going?'

She looked over her shoulder and waved.
'I'm going back,' she said. 'Don't wait for me.'
'I'm going after her,' I said.
'She must be crazy.'
Floyd grabbed hold of my arm
and stopped me.
'No!' he said. 'You can't!'

I looked at him. Was he going crazy, too?
'Wait!' he said as he watched
Karen walk away.
I saw he was shaking.
His face was white with fear.
'It's no good, Mike. Look at the snow.'

I stared in the direction
from which we had come.
I could see our footprints. Clear and crisp.
But there were only two sets.
Karen had left no footprints at all.